EVANSTON PUBLIC LIBRARY
W9-BZD-439

Sing A Song Of Sixpence

R C

Sing A Song Of Sixpence

Illustrated by
RANDOLPH CALDECOTT

Hart Publishing Company, Inc. • New York City

NEW YORK, NEW YORK 10012

ISBN NO. 08055-0359-5

MANUFACTURED IN THE UNITED STATES OF AMERICA

A Word About Randolph Caldecott

No illustrator in history has been better able to convey an expression, mood, or action in a few short strokes than Randolph Caldecott. Caldecott was born in Chester, England, in 1846. As a young man, he worked as a bank clerk in Shropshire and Manchester; his spare time, however, was completely devoted to the development of his art.

In 1872, Caldecott moved to London, where he enrolled at the famous Slade School for artists. He began illustrating children's books, and he also contributed drawings to such periodicals as *Punch* and the *Graphic.* Almost immediately, he was acclaimed as a talented and original illustrator. His unique, powerful sketches were noted for their ability to capture a personality or idiosyncracy with unequalled clarity and humor.

Although Caldecott was also an aspiring sculptor and painter, his achievements in these fields were less successful. It is solely his illustrations for which he is remembered. Indeed, his masterly drawings were often the source of a nursery story's original popularity. Such nineteenth-century favorites as "There Was An Old Woman Toss'd in a Blanket," "There Were Three Jovial Welshmen," and "A Frog He Would A-Wooing Go" are only a few of the tales which gained their widest popularity only after Caldecott had illustrated them.

Caldecott's short career had a tragic ending. At the age of thirty, his health began to deteriorate; although he did some of his best work during the next nine years, he was constantly ill during that time. His condition grew progressively worse, and finally, on February 12, 1886, he died at the age of thirty-nine.

Randolph Caldecott's legacy to us is an unparalleled collection of illustrated books which have never lost their popularity. Among them are *Old Christmas* (1876) and *Bracebridge Hall* (1877), by Washington Irving; *North Italian Folk* (1877); *The Harz Mountains* (1883); *Breton Folk* (1879); and a series of children's story-books, published between 1876 and 1886. These small works of art, including *The House that Jack Built, Death of a Mad Dog, Babes in the Woods,* and *Sing a Song of Sixpence,* are widely believed to contain Caldecott's most brilliant drawings.

NANCY GOLDBERG

Sing a Song of Sixpence,

A Pocketful

of Rye;

Four-and-Twenty Blackbirds

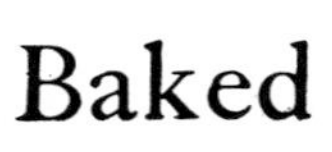

Baked

in a Pie.

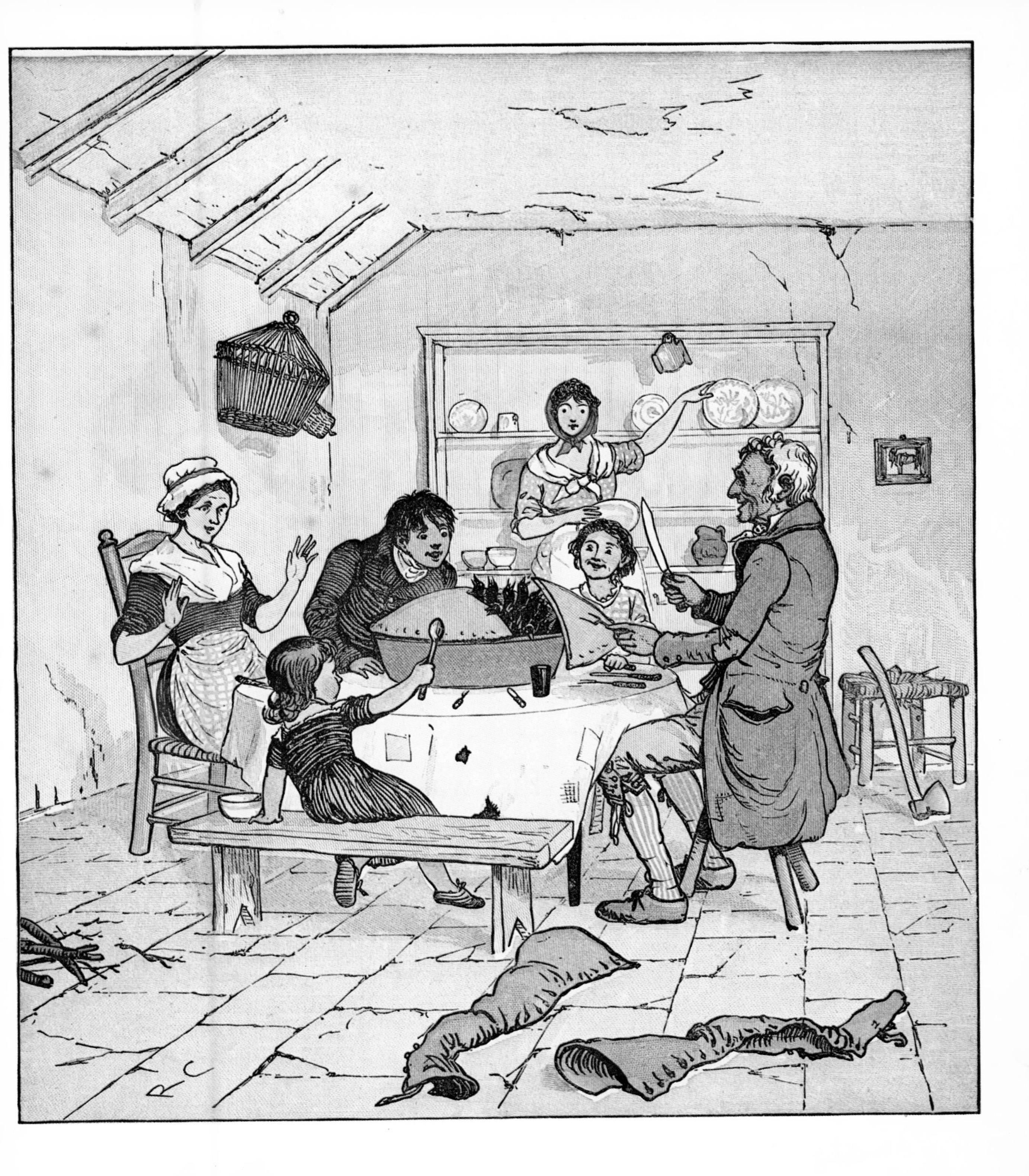

When the Pie was opened,

The Birds began to sing;

Was not that a dainty Dish

To set before the King?

The King was in

his Counting-house,

Counting out his Money.

JACK
CALENDAR

The Queen was in

the Parlor,

Eating Bread and Honey.

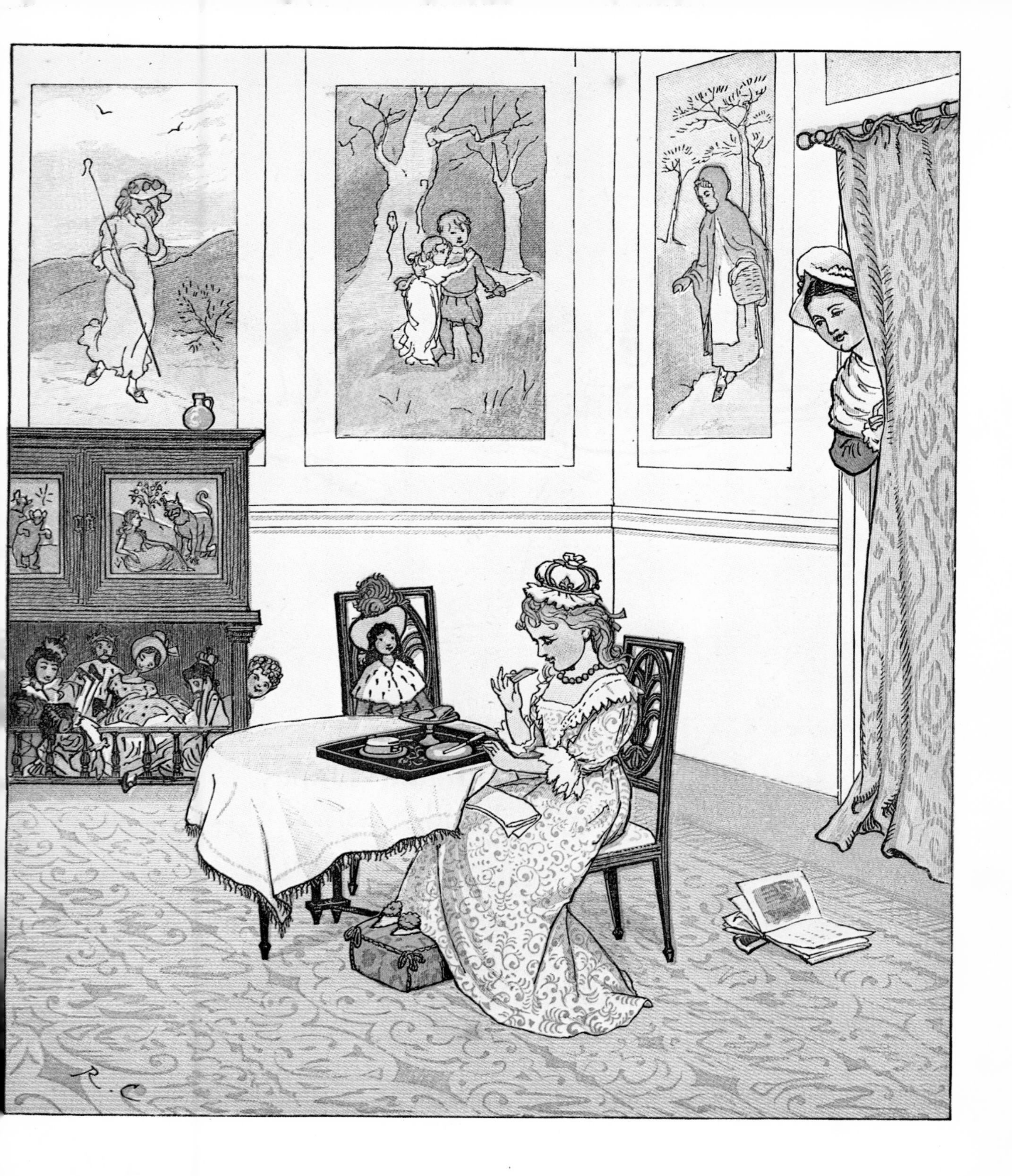
R. C

The Maid was in

the Garden,

Hanging out the Clothes;

There came a little Blackbird,

And snipped off her Nose.

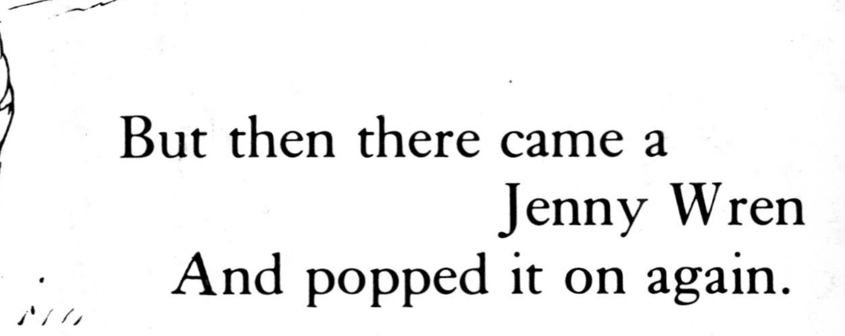

But then there came a
Jenny Wren
And popped it on again.

2884-14A
22-23